Licensed exclusively to Top That Publishing Ltd
Tide Mill Way, Woodbridge, Suffolk, IP12 1AP, UK
www.topthatpublishing.com
Copyright © 2015 Tide Mill Media
All rights reserved
2 4 6 8 9 7 5 3 1
Manufactured in China

Written by Clement C. Moore
Cover illustrated by Marcello Corti
Pages illustrated by Marcin Nowakowski

ISBN 978-1-78445-346-6

A catalogue record for this book is available from the British Library

The Night Before Christmas

An adaptation of
Clement C. Moore's famous poem

'Twas the night before Christmas,
when all through the house

Not a creature was stirring,
not even a mouse.

The stockings were hung
by the chimney with care,

In hopes that St Nicholas
soon would be there.

My sister and I were nestled
all snug in our beds,

While visions of sugar-plums
danced in our heads.

And mamma in her pyjamas,
and father in his cap,

Had just settled down for
a long winter's nap.

When out on the lawn
there arose such a clatter,

I sprang from the bed
to see what was the matter.

Away to the window
I flew like a flash,

Tore open the curtains
and threw up the sash.

The moon shining onto
the new-fallen snow
Gave the lustre of midday
to objects below.

When, what to my wondering eyes
should appear,
But a bright red sleigh,
and eight bright-eyed reindeer.

With a jolly old driver, so lively and quick,
I knew in a moment it must be St Nick.

More rapid than eagles
his reindeer they came,
And he whistled, and shouted,
and called them by name!

'Now Dasher!
Now, Dancer!
Now, Prancer
and Vixen!

On, Comet!
On, Cupid!
On, Donner
and Blitzen!

To the top of the porch!
To the top of the wall!

Now dash away! Dash away!

As dry leaves that before
the wild hurricane fly,

When they meet with an obstacle,
rising up in the sky.

So up to the house-top
the reindeers they flew,

With the sleigh full of toys,
and St Nicholas too.

Then, in a twinkling,
I heard on the roof

The prancing and pawing
of each reindeer hoof.

As I drew in my head,
and was turning around,

Down the chimney
St Nicholas came
with a bound.

He was dressed all in red,
from his head to his foot,

And his clothes were all tarnished
with ashes and soot.

A bundle of toys
he had flung on his back,

And he looked like a peddler,
just opening his pack.

His eyes – how they twinkled!
His dimples, how merry!

His cheeks were like roses,
his nose like a cherry!

His friendly mouth was
drawn up like a bow,

And the beard of his chin
was as white as the snow.

He had a broad face
and a little round belly,

That shook when he laughed,
like a bowl full of jelly!

He was chubby and plump,
a right jolly old elf,

And I laughed when I saw him,
in spite of myself!

A wink of his eye
and a twist of his head,

Soon let me know
I had nothing to dread.

He spoke not a word,
but went straight to his work,

And filled all the stockings,
then turned with a jerk.

And laying his finger
on the side of his nose,

And giving a nod,
up the chimney he rose!

He sprang to his sleigh,
to his team gave a whistle,

And away they all flew
like the seeds of a thistle.

But I heard him exclaim,
before he drove out of sight,

'Happy Christmas to all,

and to all a good-night!"

Christmas Traditions
from Around the World

Christmas Crackers

In the *UK*, Christmas crackers are usually pulled during Christmas dinner. Crackers normally have a paper hat, a joke and a small toy or gift inside.

Saint Nicholas

In *Germany*, on the 6th December, Saint Nicholas visits small children and will often put sweets in their shoes if they have been good that year.

Stockings

In the *United States*, it is a tradition for children to hang stockings on the fireplace for Santa Claus to fill with presents while they are sleeping on Christmas night.

La Cabalgata

On the 5th January, in many *Spanish* cities, they have a parade (La Cabalgata), which welcomes the Three Kings to the city. The Kings often throw sweets to the children in the crowd.

La Guadalupana

In *Mexico*, the Christmas celebrations begin on the 12th December, where they have a feast of La Guadalupana, and end on the 6th January with the Epiphany.

7th January

In *Russia*, Christmas Day is celebrated on the 7th January because of a difference between the new Gregorian and older Julian calendars.

Christmas Eve

The main day for celebration in *Norway* is on Christmas Eve. Many people will attend a church service and then eat their main Christmas dinner that evening, before opening their presents.

If you enjoyed The Night Before Christmas, why not try When I dream of Christmas, a humorous look at Christmas traditions.

ISBN: 978-1-78700-009-4
EAN: 9 781849 567268